55 FRIENDS

# 55 FRIENDS

ABBIE ZABAR

HYPERION BOOKS FOR CHILDREN
NEW YORK

For information address Hyperion Books for Children,
114 Fifth Avenue, New York, NY 10011.

A different version of *55 Friends*
originally appeared as a Read-Aloud story in *Child* magazine.

First Edition
1  3  5  7  9  10  8  6  4  2

Library of Congress Cataloging-in-Publication Data

Zabar, Abbie.
55 friends/Abbie Zabar — 1st ed.
p.  cm.
Summary: In a land called Save-the-Day, fifty-five unlikely
creatures share a friendship and demonstrate counting from
one to ten.
ISBN 0-7868-0021-6
[1. Animals — Fiction. 2. Friendship — Fiction. 3. Counting.]
I. Title. II. Title: Fifty-five friends.
PZ7.Z13Aaf 1994
[E] — dc20  93-47366   CIP    AC

The artwork for this book is prepared using pen and ink,
colored pencils and markers, and paper collage.
All of the text is hand lettered.

A million thanks to these 14 friends who helped with

## 55 FRIENDS

Andrea Cascardi and Kristen Behrens and Mary Beth Jordan and
Mary Flower and Ellen Friedman and Juli Barbato and Linda Prather
and Connie Hahn and Alan Heller and Anne-Marie Colban and
Sally Schermerhorn and Mary Ehni and Yolanda Beltran and
Timothy!

Peace on Earth & Good will toward men

AND ALL THE REST OF US

THANK YOU

Once upon a time,
long ago and far away
in a land called Save-the-Day,

there was 1 worm...

Squirmy but firm.

Once upon a time,
long ago and far away
in a land called Save-the-Day,
there were

2 Shoe-flies in bow ties

and

1 worm ... Squirmy but firm.

Once upon a time,
long ago and far away
in a land called Save-the-Day,
there were
3 bees busy buzzing
and
2 shoe-flies in bow ties and
1 worm... squirmy but firm.

Once upon a time,
long ago and far away
in a land called Save-the-Day,
there were
4 nevermore dinosaurs
and
3 bees busy buzzing and
2 shoe-flies in bow ties and
1 worm... squirmy but firm.

Once upon a time,
long ago and far away
in a land called Save-the-Day,
there were
5 butter-colored flutter-byes
and
4 nevermore dinosaurs and
3 bees busy buzzing and
2 shoe-flies in bow ties and
1 worm ... squirmy but firm.

Once upon a time,
long ago and far away
in a land called Save-the-Day,

there were

6 fly-by-night bats
and

5 butter-colored flutter-byes and

4 nevermore dinosaurs and

3 bees busy buzzing and

2 shoe-flies in bow ties and

1 worm ... squirmy but firm.

Once upon a time,
long ago and far away
in a land called Save-the-Day,
there were

7 silly salamanders and
6 fly-by-night bats and
5 butter-colored flutter-byes and
4 nevermore dinosaurs and
3 bees busy buzzing and
2 shoe-flies in bow ties and
1 worm... Squirmy but firm.

Once upon a time,
long ago and far away
in a land called Save-the-Day,
there were
8 fancy-schmancy ants
and

7 silly salamanders and

6 fly-by-night bats and

5 butter-colored flutter-byes and

4 nevermore dinosaurs and

3 bees busy buzzing and

2 shoe-flies in bow ties and

1 worm...squirmy but firm"

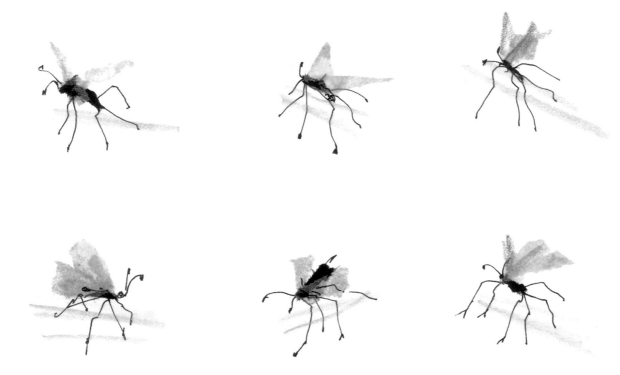

Once upon a time,
long ago and far away
in a land called Save-the-Day,
there were
9 neat gnats
and
8 fancy-schmancy ants and
7 silly salamanders and
6 fly-by-night bats and
5 butter-colored flutter-byes and
4 nevermore dinosaurs and
3 bees busy buzzing and
2 shoe-flies in bow ties and
1 worm... squirmy but firm.

Once upon a time,

long ago and far away

in a land called

Save-the-Day,

there were

10 Tom cats

and 9 neat  and

8 fancy-schmancy and 7 silly

and 6 fly-by-night

and 5 butter-colored

and 4 nevermore

and 3 busy buzzing and 2 in bow ties

and 1 ... squirmy but firm.

And they lived happily ever after.

BECAUSE FRIENDS WON'T ALL LOOK ALIKE, THANK YOU!